Madison in
Manhattan

By Amy McCready

Illustrated By Chrissie Dowler

Printed in the United States of America

Summary: Madison lives in Manhattan with her owner, Amy, where she loves exploring the sights and sounds of the City. In this adventure to Central Park, Madison learns that sharing is important.

Library of Congress Control Number: 2008902957

ISBN 978-0-9816549-0-4

Lady Maddog LLC

www.madisonthedog.com

ladymaddog@nyc.rr.com

For John

"Good morning, Madison!" Amy says in her "it's-a-great-day" voice. Amy knows a cheerful voice helps Madison wake up. Barely opening her eyes, Madison peers up at Amy without moving from underneath the covers.

A few more minutes of sleeping would be nice, Madison thinks to herself. "Did you sleep well last night?" asks Amy. She sees Madison is going to need some convincing this morning to wake up. She has never met a dog so content to stay in bed.

"Alright, Maddie-dog. It's time to get out of bed!" Amy declares in her most serious and stern motherly voice. She pulls the blanket off Madison and nudges her gently.

Madison seems particulary bothered by Amy's nudging but soon realizes it is time to get up.

Her mouth erupts into a big yawn, and she slowly crawls out of bed.

"Good girl, Maddie. Now let's do some stretches before we go to the…" Amy stops mid-sentence to get Madison's attention.

Madison's ears perk up waiting to hear where they are going. She loves to go everywhere, but she hopes Amy is going to say that wonderful word, that glorious place, which is her very favorite place to go.

"... PARK!" Amy finishes with a big smile.
Madison LOVES the park! When she hears Amy say the word "park" her
ears stand straight up like a bunny rabbit.

Madison starts her stretching routine. She always does her stretches in the same order just like Amy taught her.

First, she stretches her shoulders and upper body.

Then she stretches her front legs. Finally, she stretches her back legs.

"Let's get ready to go," says Amy. She looks around their little
Manhattan apartment for Madison's things. "What do we need for your
walk? I'll find your collar, leash and water bowl. You pick out a toy, ok?"

$\mathcal{M}$adison charges over to her toy basket. She has so many toys that she does not know which one to choose. There's her red ball with yellow polka dots, a green bone, a yellow bone, a fuzzy lamb, an orange doggy puppet with a squeaker in his nose, her Empire State Building, a pink birthday cake and lots and lots of stuffed animals.

Finally, Madison decides on her yellow bone. She loves for Amy to throw it to her in the park.

They leave the apartment, walk to the elevator and press the down arrow button. Madison is so happy she is jumping for joy.

"I know you're excited, but we have to wait for the elevator," Amy tells Madison. When the elevator arrives and the doors begin to creak open, Madison shoves her nose through the crack and darts into the elevator. "Are you ready to go to the park?" Amy asks. Madison replies with a loud bark as they head down to the lobby.

W hen the elevator opens, Madison pushes her nose through the doors and bounds into the lobby.

"Well, good morning Madison. How are you today?" asks Nicholas, the building's doorman. Nicholas wears a black hat and white gloves. He takes care of their building.

He makes sure the building is clean…

and the mail is delivered…

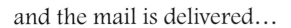

and announces visitors.

Madison likes Nicholas because he always smiles at her and pets her head very gently. Sometimes, he even gives her a treat. She LOVES treats! This morning Madison is so excited she dashes right past Nicholas out the front door. Amy waves good-bye as Madison drags her towards the park.

At the corner is their favorite deli where Amy buys her milk and cheese. Amy spots the deli cat, Calvin, sunbathing in the doorway. "Ohhh, Maddie, look! There's the kitty, Calvin."

Her ears perk up when she hears the word "kitty". She LOVES kitties! Madison barks and pulls on her leash. She wants to play with Calvin.

Calvin, enjoying the quiet of the morning, scowls at Madison's loud barking. He leaps onto the windowsill to escape the noise.

"Let's go Maddie, we have more important things to do than bother Calvin," says Amy. "Don't you want to go to the park and chase squirrels?" Madison LOVES squirrels!

Madison rushes into the street towards the park before Amy can pull back on her leash. "We have to wait for a green light!" Amy scolds her. Madison's ears go back, and she looks up at Amy with her best "I'm sorry" eyes. Amy forgives her and kisses Madison on the nose.

On the way to the park, they walk through the beautiful gardens of the American Museum of Natural History and Planetarium. The museum is across the street from Central Park.

A group of students rush out of a school bus and line up to visit the museum. "Look at all of the children, Maddie," says Amy. "They're going to see the dinosaurs."

"Look Maddie, there's the park!" Amy exclaims. In her excitement, Madison begins jumping all over the sidewalk, on Amy,

on the old lady sitting on the bench, on anyone who will share in her joy that she made it to the PARK!

Madison is so excited she almost runs into the ice cream man who is setting up his cart full of treats.

CENTRAL
PARK

ICE
CREAM

She can barely control herself. Madison wants to run around with the other dogs. They are chasing squirrels and playing. "Run, Maddie, run!" Amy shouts. Madison races down the dirt path towards all the other dogs. Suddenly, she stops and turns around to make sure Amy is close behind her. She sees Amy and feeling safe turns back around and dashes deeper into the park.

Madison is on a mission… a mission to find squirrels. She spots two playing in the green grass and races after them.

She chases the squirrels up the tree and circles the trunk sniffing the ground. "Maddie, those squirrels are scared of you," Amy declares.

M adison, feeling very important now, struts off down the path...

looking for more trouble.

Amy and Madison walk quietly through the park enjoying the sunshine and all the park activities around them.

Eventually, they sit down on a large rock overlooking all the runners, bikers, families and other dogs enjoying the beautiful day. "Thirsty, Maddie?" Madison eagerly drinks the water from her little bowl.

"Look, is that Sofie?" Amy asks.

Across the lawn, they see Sofie, a black Labrador, galloping towards them with Ralphie, her purple duck, in her mouth.

Madison jumps up and runs towards her. They roll in the grass and chase each other in circles.

Suddenly, Madison lunges at Sofie and grabs Ralphie. Poor little Ralphie is now the center of a mean tug-of-war game! "No Maddie," exclaims Amy. "That is not how you play with Sofie. Let go of Ralphie!"

Madison does not share well with other dogs. She thinks every toy should belong to her. Amy wants Madison to learn how to share toys because sharing is the right thing to do.

Amy throws Madison's yellow bone across the lawn. Madison, seeing her bone flying through the air, lets go of Ralphie to fetch her toy.

"Now, Maddie if you want to play with Ralphie, you should let Sofie play with your yellow bone." Madison is not so sure she wants to give Sofie her yellow bone... but she really wants to play with Ralphie.

Madison walks over to Sofie and drops her bone. Sofie wags her tail and pushes Ralphie to Madison. Amy smiles. She is so proud of Madison for sharing. "Good girl!" Amy says.

The two friends settle down together with their toys in the grass.

$\mathcal{S}$oon it is time to leave the park. Amy and Madison gather their things and say goodbye to Sofie. They walk back to their apartment. On their way, they pass the ice cream man, the old lady on the bench, and all the children leaving the museum.

They walk by Sammy's Deli where Calvin is napping on the windowsill.

Back at their building, Nicholas is waiting for Madison. He gives her a treat. Madison LOVES treats!

$\mathcal{A}$my and Madison ride up the elevator and walk into their cool, little Manhattan apartment. Tired from their trip to the park, they head straight to the sofa. Madison curls up next to Amy, closes her eyes and dreams about chasing squirrels.